CATSWALK

Trina Robbins

CATSWALK
The Growing of Girl

TRINA ROBBINS

CELESTIAL ARTS

Berkeley, California

Thank you to Steve, Caryn, Sal, and Cynthia
for your criticism, praise, encouragement, and suggestions.

CELESTIAL ARTS
P. O. Box 7327
Berkeley, California 94707

Cover design by Ken Scott
Text design by Faith and Folly
Author photo by Mark Leialoha
Set in Novarese and Lithos

Library of Congress Cataloging-in-Publication Data

Robbins, Trina
    Catswalk : the growing of Girl / written and illustrated by Trina Robbins.
       p.   cm.
    Summary: In ancient Mesopotamia, Girl embarks on a journey of self-discovery
with the giant speaking cat who has raised her.
     ISBN 0-89087-608-8
     [1. Cat — Fiction. 2. Fantasy.]   I. Title.
   PZ7.R5382Cat   1990
[Fic] — dc20   90-44351
                                            CIP
                                            AC

First Printing, 1990

Manufactured in the United States of America

1 2 3 4 5 — 94 93 92 91 90

For Casey, my own Girl

SO VERY LONG AGO THAT THERE WAS ALMOST NO HISTORY yet, a young girl and a talking cat lived in a small hut by a river. The extremely large cat had a coat of thick gray fur, and her name was Mother. She was the only mother the girl had ever known.

The girl's dark eyes shone with the color of ripe blackberries. Her hair, which matched her eyes, hung free about her shoulders. Her skin was tanned by the sun that blazed overhead in a cloudless sky.

Sometimes Mother called the girl "my little fish." This was because one day, when Mother had been fishing in the river ("Because we cats *do* love fish, you know."), who should float by but the girl, who was then a tiny baby. Mother pulled her out and raised her. Of course, the girl didn't remember any of this.

Mostly, the large gray cat called her Girl, so this was the name she had.

Their little, round hut was built of the reeds that grew at the water's edge. The walls, plastered with mud from the riverbanks, didn't have to keep out the cold because there was no winter in this land. Occasionally it rained, and the thickly thatched roof kept the room cozy and dry. A hole in the center of the ceiling let out smoke from the open hearth, and at night Girl looked right through the hole at the moon and stars.

In front of the hut, a small patch of earth was planted with barley and lentils, lettuce, cucumbers, and melons. Chickens scratched near the door, and farther away a small goat was tethered to a date palm.

And farther yet, the brown and muddy river stretched from one end of Girl's world to the other. Mother told Girl that the river was called the Euphrates, but she and the other folk who lived on its banks thought of it as simply "the river."

Sometimes rafts floated by, and great cargo ships, loaded with huge cedar logs that were destined to become pillars of some great house, headed for the city in the North. But Girl had been nowhere except the lands around her home.

On either side of the river lay a vast plain, flat and brown as the water except for a broad strip that followed the banks, where all manner of water plants and palm trees grew. If Girl squinted, she could just make out the faint outlines of mountains.

Girl did not know that living with a large talking cat was anything unusual. Indeed, their days by the river were very ordinary.

Mother did all the things a mother is supposed to do for her daughter. While Girl scattered seed for the chickens and milked the goat, Mother weeded the garden and spun the goat's fleece into yarn. She swept the floor with a broom of rushes, washed Girl's only other dress, taught her good manners, scolded her, and loved her.

And Mother made the most delicious barley cakes, dotted with raisins and flavored with honey from a nearby hive. At night, she and Girl ate those cakes with cheese and washed down with milk, both provided by the same little goat. After dinner, Girl would sit by the hearth and listen to Mother tell stories, or they would play at riddles and guessing games.

Sometimes Mother would tell her about the Catswalk. "It's something that every cat must do at least once in life," she said. "We just set out and walk somewhere—anywhere—to see what we may see."

Girl was impressed with all that Mother knew. She thought no wiser cat existed in the world. "Are you the First Cat?" she asked.

Mother shook her head and the firelight danced in her green eyes. "No, but my great-grandmother was the First Cat, and I am the last of the Great Cats."

One night after eating, Girl and Mother sat by the fire telling riddles. Mother would ask one for Girl to guess, and then it would be Girl's turn.

"What can you keep," asked Girl, "even after giving it to someone else?"

"Not hard to answer," replied Mother. "My word. Now tell me what has a mouth but never eats, a bed but never sleeps?"

Girl looked out the open door at the water which reflected the stars as it flowed by. "A river!" she shouted.

Then she saw something else through the doorway. In the distance, walking alongside the river toward the hut, was a man! His back bowed under the weight of the immense pack strapped to his shoulders, and he leaned on a walking stick. Girl could tell he was weary.

Mother saw the traveller at the same time. "Well," she exclaimed, "we're about to have a visitor!" She quickly groomed herself, licking her front paw and washing her face and ears so as to look presentable.

Girl bustled about, tidying the little room, while Mother put a great kettle on the fire. "He'll be hungry," she said. "Tired, but especially hungry."

How excited Girl was! It wasn't often that anyone passed their way, and every visitor was an adventure. By now the stranger stood in the doorway, and though the door was open, he rapped politely on the door frame.

"Good evening," he called. "May a weary traveller find a warm hearth here, with perhaps a crust of bread and a night's rest?"

Just as politely, Mother bade him enter. "All strangers are welcome in this humble dwelling, and what little we have is shared gladly."

Girl knew that Mother was being modest, because the Great Cat was quite proud of their neat little home and most certainly did not consider it humble. Girl studied their guest as he shrugged out of his pack with a relieved sigh. Oh, this one was from very far away! He was small, thin, and copper colored, unlike the sturdy olive-skinned folk she knew. And his clothing was different. He wore leather sandals, etched with golden designs, and a pleated linen skirt. His chest was bare, but around his neck hung a blue, beaded collar so wide it formed a capelet over his shoulders. Although more pleated linen covered his head, Girl could see that he was shaved quite bald. And around his eyes he had drawn a thick black line, making them resemble Mother's.

Just now those eyes smiled at Girl, for he had noticed her watching him. "Surely this must be a magic palace, enchanted to look like a hut," he said. "For behold! A princess greets me!" And, before Girl could say a thing, he kissed her hand. "I am Ramose, a simple merchant from a distant land, and ever at your service."

Turning to look at Mother, his expression changed to one of reverence. Bowing low, Ramose said, "Forgive me, Madame. In the smoke from the fire, at first I did not see clearly . . . Have I the honor of addressing one of the Great Cats?"

Mother was charmed and offered her paw to be pressed against his forehead. "I see you are a man of much learning," she murmured.

"Even in my faraway country, we know of the Great Cats. Yet I have never before met one."

Girl offered the merchant a bowl of dates. "Mother is the last of the Great Cats," she explained.

If Ramose thought it odd that a young girl should refer to such a fabled creature as Mother, he said nothing. Instead, addressing Mother again, he asked, "May I inquire of your name?"

"I have had many names," answered the Great Cat. "But as you can see," inclining her head toward Girl, "I am these days known as Mother."

"Alas, it has been many years since I have had a mother," said the merchant. "So if I may, respectfully I will refer to you as Madame."

After consuming two steaming bowls of Mother's lentil stew, Ramose took a turn at regaling the girl and the Great Cat with riddles and stories of his travels. He sat before the hearth, and the flames outlined his body in gold and cast his face into deep shadow. With tail curled around her and paws neatly tucked under, Mother lay facing him. Girl, her arm around Mother's warm gray neck, sat entranced as he spoke.

"A Great Cat lives in my country, even larger than you, Madame," Ramose nodded to Mother, "but not as kind. For she sits in the desert, waiting for unwary wanderers to pass, and to these she poses riddles. Those who can answer her riddles she allows to proceed, even rewarding them with gold and precious jewels. But to those who have no answer, guess what she does?"

"What does she do?" asked Girl.

"She gobbles them right up!" And Ramose pounced on Girl, pretending to eat her and frightening her at first, but then reducing her to a fit of giggles so that she almost choked on the date she was eating.

Mother's whiskers twitched indignantly. "That is no Great Cat! We Great Cats never eat people!"

"Forgive me, Madame," said Ramose gravely. "You are right. The creature of whom I speak is a sphinx, and I am happy to say that I have never met her.

"Still," he added, "it is a good thing to know the answers to riddles." And he proceeded to tell them riddles until Girl fell asleep, curled up on a nest of fleecy, white sheepskin by the hearth.

Girl was awakened at sunrise by the rooster's crow. Upon opening her eyes she saw that Ramose and Mother had already been up for some time. They were sitting by the hearth, sipping Mother's morning tea, which she made from roasted barley and wild cherry bark, flavored with cinnamon and honey. Girl ran outside and washed her face in the big basin of rainwater that stood by the door. Then she hurried inside to join them.

Ramose greeted her. "Well, here's the princess, and she has brought me breakfast."

"But I haven't brought you anything," Girl protested, thinking, I hope I haven't disappointed him.

The merchant placed his hand over her left ear and drew out—an egg! Puzzled, Girl felt her ear. Surely she hadn't had an egg in there.

"One for me," Ramose announced. Then, from her right ear, he drew forth another egg. "And one for the princess."

"Are you a magician, sir?" Girl asked.

"Of sorts." Then he peered at her arm. "Why, you've something up your sleeve!"

"I do?" Girl reached up her sleeve but could feel nothing there.

"No, no, allow me," he said, and reaching into Girl's sleeve, Ramose slowly pulled out a long scarf of sheerest silk. Girl caught her breath. The scarf was beautiful! The soft bands of color blended into one another so that it looked like

a rainbow when Ramose waved it through the air. He bowed at the waist and presented it to her.

"Rainbows such as this, princess, should not be hidden in a sleeve."

Girl had never owned anything so bright. Her own two dresses were of undyed fleece. When she knotted the scarf about her slender waist, she felt she wore all the colors in the world.

Meanwhile, Mother had been frying the two eggs in a copper pan and now served them on clay plates, along with two bowls of porridge. Between bites, the merchant explained that he was on his way to the city to trade the wares he carried.

"Please allow me to make some poor payment for my meals, my bed, and your delightful company, ladies," he said, unrolling his great pack.

"Little princess, I beg you to pick a trinket, any trinket, and it is yours." He gestured at the sparkling gewgaws which tumbled out onto the dirt floor. "Jewels from a queen's treasure box! Sapphires that reflect the sky, little princess. Rubies like drops of blood; an emerald from the eyes of a terrible golden god! Cunning monkeys, carved of ivory, white as your smile. Drops of the sun itself, melted into brazen bangles! Tell me your pleasure."

Girl hesitated. The little pile of treasures shone more brightly than the rainbow-colored scarf about her waist. How could she choose? Then Mother reached over and picked up something. She held the object to the fire so Girl could see the glow of flames right through it. Translucent amber, carved into a curious form! Girl examined it more closely as it lay in Mother's paw.

"Why, it's shaped like a cat! A cat that looks very much like you, Mother!" The amber was on a long golden chain and could be worn around the neck. "It's different from the others. How strange. I didn't see it because the shine from all the other jewels blinded me."

"This is the one she needs," Mother stated matter-of-factly, slipping the amulet over Girl's head. At once Girl's neck tingled.

The merchant bowed low to Mother. "The Great Cat makes a wise choice."

Then he straightened and refilled his pack with the spilled jewels. "And now I must take leave of your charming company. For the city, you know, will not come to the merchant, so the merchant must go to the city."

"I'd like to see the city someday," Girl mused.

"And perhaps you will, someday," answered Ramose, bidding them good-bye.

Girl was sorry to see him go. She and Mother had so few visitors. She waved to him until he passed out of sight. Then she sighed and headed back to the hut. After all, she thought, there are many things to do today. The chickens must be fed, the goat must be milked . . .

As Girl entered the hut, something caught her eye. A beam of light, shining through the hole in the roof, illuminated a rolled-up parchment that lay in the middle of the floor so it seemed to glow. Ramose must have left it! She picked it up and ran to show Mother.

Mother studied the parchment. "It's a map," she declared, handing it back to Girl. "Run and see if you can find the merchant. I'm sure this is important to him."

Girl ran outside, clutching the map tightly. Ramose was gone. She followed his footprints along the sandy riverside and up a little rise. But once on the other side of the rise, she could see nothing but smooth sand. The footprints had vanished.

"Well!" exclaimed Mother, when Girl returned with the news. "WELL!" again. She licked a paw and smoothed down a whisker. Finally she said, "We must find the merchant and return his map. Without it, surely he will get lost on the great plain that stretches beyond the river.

"Anyway," she added, while drawing on her shawl, "it is time we went on a Catswalk."

MOTHER BAKED UP A BIG BATCH OF BARLEY CAKES
and Girl filled a basket with goat cheese and dates. Then Mother
packed her best shiny copper pot and the two fine, red clay bowls, painted with
little animals. Carefully, Girl bundled up her other dress and rolled their
sleeping mats. Mother swept the floor of the hut one last time.

"So it will be presentable for the next person," she said, shutting the door
firmly. Outside, she surveyed the chickens critically as they clucked and pecked
at seed. She sighed. "I suppose they'll be all right."

Girl felt her chest tighten with anxiety. "Mother, aren't we coming back?"

Mother was tying their baggage onto the little goat's back. "Maybe yes," she
replied, "maybe no. That's how a Catswalk is."

Leading the patient goat, they walked away from the only home Girl had
ever known. Girl tried to look forward to the adventure that lay ahead. After all,
Mother says it's time for a Catswalk, and she *is* the last Great Cat, so she must
know. Nevertheless, every few steps Girl turned and looked back wistfully at the
little house until, finally, when she turned, she could no longer see it. But
Mother never looked back at all.

Walking was easy. They followed the river north as the merchant had done, towards the mountains, which loomed, purple and misty, always far in the distance. All around them, the land was flat and brown, except next to the river where groves of date palms and wild bananas grew. Reeds and papyrus thrust up from the marshy riverside. Sometimes their approach startled the flocks of geese who made their homes among the water plants.

When they stopped for lunch, Girl studied the map. She called the great gray cat over. "Look, Mother. This long wavy line is the river. And see? Wherever there's a tiny drawing of palm trees, that means there's an oasis. And these little houses must mean a village is located there.

"But what can these strange markings mean? They're all over the map."

Mother pointed to the markings with her graceful paw. "That is called writing," she explained. "If you can read it, my little fish, it will give you important information. And sometimes it tells you stories, like I do at night."

"Can a parchment tell stories?" Girl marvelled. "I wish I could read."

"I can't read," said Mother. "Great Cats don't need to read. However, you must learn. Still," she added, "we can follow the map."

And, using the map, they followed the river all the rest of that day. Twice, rafts floated by and swarthy, bearded men on board waved to the two travellers. But no sign of the merchant did they see. When it grew dark, they tied the goat to a palm tree that was surrounded by good green grass for her to munch. They had nothing to cook, but the barley cakes were delicious, and Mother brewed an herb tea to keep away the evening's chill.

Girl hadn't realized how tired she was. She cuddled up against Mother's warm, soft body and fell asleep right after dinner. But Mother pulled her shawl more tightly about her furry shoulders and sat up, watching the stars.

On the third day of their journey they met the boy.

With her superior cat's eyes, Mother saw him first from far off, but she said nothing. Then Girl saw him. He was sitting against a palm tree by the side of the

footpath. As the girl and the gray cat approached, he barely glanced at them, and then turned away as if he hadn't noticed them at all.

Girl had been trained by Mother to be polite. She walked over to the boy and greeted him. "Good day. Are you travelling far?"

The boy yawned elaborately and inspected his fingernails. "Yes," he replied shortly.

How insulting! Girl thought. After all, it's true that I'm just a young girl who's never been anywhere before, but you'd think he'd see that Mother is a Great Cat. But she persisted in being polite. "Mother and I are stopping for lunch now. Would you care to join us?"

"No," replied the boy, causing Girl to become more irritated than ever. He hadn't even said thank you!

Girl shrugged. She and Mother spread a cloth under a nearby palm tree, and on it they arranged the goat cheese and barley cakes in the two clay bowls and a basket of dates.

Perhaps, thought Girl bitterly as she took a big bite of cheese, this food isn't good enough for him. No doubt he comes from the city and is used to much more wonderful dishes than simple barley cakes.

But then she noticed the boy watching them out of the corner of his eye and licking his lips. Why, she realized, he's only *pretending* not to be interested! He's probably famished!

Mother had noticed, too. "Oh, my," she said loudly, "I've just baked up a new batch of barley cakes, and I can't tell if they're any good. I may have added too much salt."

She turned to the boy. "Young man, would you mind kindly testing this cake and giving me your opinion?"

The boy sauntered over beneath the tree and took the cake Mother offered. He took a little nibble, and then, before he remembered that he wasn't supposed to be hungry, he stuffed the entire cake into his mouth, chewed it up, and swallowed it!

"It's perfectly good," he told Mother. He took the second cake that Mother held out to him and devoured it in only two bites. "Very good," he added, his mouth full of barley cake.

His terrible manners shocked Girl. Mother had taught her not to speak with a full mouth. Perhaps we should introduce ourselves, she thought, when he's through chewing, that is.

"I'm Girl," she began, "and this is Mother. She . . ."

"Girl! Is *that* your name?"

More bad manners, thought Girl. She was embarrassed for him. "Well, that's the only name I have."

"But," exclaimed the boy, "the only name I have is Boy!" Then he took another barley cake from the bowl, without asking permission, and leaned against the tree.

"I come from the city, and I've never had a family or home. I've never had a name, either, and everyone has always simply called me Boy."

"As long as I can remember," he continued, "I've stolen food from the bazaars when I was hungry and curled up to sleep with the other homeless boys in doorways or corners. But the other homeless boys had real names, and they made fun of me because the only name I had was Boy."

That explains his terrible manners, Girl realized. The poor thing never had a mother to teach him how to behave properly.

The boy had finished with the barley cakes. He was licking the crumbs from the corners of his mouth and eyeing the dates hungrily. Mother pushed the basket towards him.

"Well, maybe just one," he said, taking a handful. "I heard stories," he went on, as he stuffed his mouth with dates, "stories of heroes who earned great names for themselves by doing great deeds—names like 'Lion Slayer' or 'King Maker.' And I resolved that I, too, would become a hero and earn a great name."

Now he started on the goat cheese. "When I go back to the city with a name like 'Serpent Killer' or 'Swift Foot,' *then* let's see them laugh! And so I've left the city to wander in search of adventure." Boy sighed. "I've been wandering for almost a week now, and you're the first adventure I've found," he concluded.

Upon closer examination, Girl saw that Boy was about the same size as she, and looked to be about the same age, but the resemblance ended there. His hair, though the same dark color as hers, badly needed washing and

combing. In fact, the entire boy needed washing. His roughly woven tunic and cloak were badly worn, too, and in need of patches. He might not be so awful looking after a bath, she decided, except his ears stuck out way too much.

"I could come along with you," Boy suggested hopefully, "to protect you against fierce beasts. You know, like lions and such."

"Well, if that isn't the silliest . . ." began Girl. The only beasts they had seen in three days were the rabbits that peered timidly from the tall grasses as they passed, or the ducks and geese waddling by the riverside.

But Mother interrupted her. "Oh, *lions*. Of course we'll need protection from *lions*. Please do come along." And solemnly she winked one great green eye at Girl.

Boy faltered. "Uh, just where *are* you going, exactly?"

Girl had tucked the map into her rainbow sash. She unrolled it and showed it to Boy, explaining about Ramose. "I don't suppose you've seen him?"

Boy shook his head. "I've seen no one but the two of you. But I'll bet he's gone to the city. Everyone goes to the city."

"See, here it is," he indicated on the map, "that big square."

Then he looked at the map more closely. "Why, there are *many* cities on the map, and I thought mine was the only city!"

But Girl was looking at something else. The writing—right on the spot next to the river and by the oasis, right where they were probably standing at this minute—she understood what it said!

"B-O-Y," she read laboriously. "It says, BOY HERE."

GIRL SQUINTED AND FROWNED, TURNING THE PARCH-
ment this way and that, but except for the words BOY HERE, she couldn't make out the rest of the writing. Finally she rolled the map back up and tucked it into her sash.

The following day, Mother and Girl added another member to their group. It was late morning, and they had been walking since their sunrise breakfast. Soon the sun would be directly overhead in the cloudless sky, and already the dusty earth of the footpath felt hot beneath Girl's bare feet. In just a little while they would stop for lunch.

The travellers were passing low outcroppings of rock where grasses grew sparsely when Girl stopped suddenly.

"Listen," she called out, "someone is crying!"

Could it be a baby? But it wasn't a human. Boy heard it, too. He searched among the low rocks.

"It's coming from this direction. Look, there's a little cave down here." He got down on his knees and peered through the tiny opening. "Oh!" he exclaimed, and reached in. When he drew his hand back out, he held a little, brown, furry four-legged creature.

"Poor thing, it's shivering," cried Girl. "But what is it?"

"It's a puppy," Boy told her. "A boy puppy. Haven't you ever seen one before?"

"I guess not. But where's its mother?"

Mother was looking at markings on the ground behind some rocks and spoke quietly. "I don't think its mother will be coming back."

The children climbed over the rocks to see. There were paw prints in the dirt, like Mother's, only much, much bigger.

"Lion." Mother said just the one word.

Girl shivered. So there really were lions here! And then she realized what Mother was saying. Poor puppy. It was an orphan.

The puppy sat in Boy's cupped hands, where it fit perfectly. It whined and licked his fingers. Then it peered up at Girl timidly with brown eyes that took up almost half of its tiny head. Gently, she petted the top of its head, and the brown baby fur was even softer than Mother's.

"Oh, Mother, isn't it pretty? I think it's hungry."

Mother grumbled. "Another mouth to feed. And I suppose I know who'll do the feeding. What shall it be next, a baby elephant?" But she dug out a barley cake from her basket and fed it to the puppy who gobbled it down zestfully.

Boy carried the little creature all day, except when they stopped to rest. Then he let it down, and while they sat in the shade of a tree, the puppy dashed into the underbrush on its stubby legs, pretending to chase rabbits. Then it would trot back, yipping happily, and lick Boy's hand. That night, it snuggled up to sleep with Boy.

Before she closed her eyes, Girl unrolled the map to take one more look by the flickering firelight. Drawn on the parchment was the group of trees that represented the oasis where they were camped for the night. Halfway between that spot and the place they slept the night before a tiny cave was drawn. She drew in her breath sharply. Right over the cave were markings she could read: PLACE OF THE PUP.

As the small group moved on, Mother tried unsuccessfully to teach Boy manners. It seemed he was always hungry and had a habit of grabbing for food

without ever saying "please" or "may I." Mother complained that he and the puppy ate enough to feed an army of giants, and indeed the puppy grew into a young dog almost overnight.

About the only success Mother had was in getting Boy clean. He soon discovered what fun it was to swim in the river with his new dog friend. Girl liked to join them, for swimming was the perfect way to cool off when the day grew too hot. But Mother didn't like water at all. While they swam, she sat on the bank and groomed herself meticulously, using her rough pink tongue and her velvety paws.

Boy and the dog had become special friends, and soon the dog earned a name. When Boy tossed a stick into the air, the dog ran to fetch it eagerly, sometimes catching it in midair. Then he would deposit the stick at Boy's feet and wait, panting happily, until his friend called him "good dog" and threw it again. And so, Boy named the dog Fetcher.

When the travellers stopped for food or rest, Boy and Fetcher would trot off out of sight to play together. One day Boy ran back with Fetcher at his heels.

"Girl," he called, "I've taught Fetcher a new game! Come see!"

Girl stood up reluctantly and joined them. She thought Boy's games were silly.

Boy was excited. "Give me something of yours," he commanded. "Here, your sash! That will do."

"Well . . . promise you'll give it back?"

"Don't be silly. Now go hide somewhere. Go on, anywhere!"

Shrugging, Girl crouched behind some bushes a good distance away and peered out between the leaves. Boy, who had been shielding Fetcher's eyes, now held the sash to the dog's nose. Fetcher sniffed noisily. "Go find her, Fetcher!"

Then Fetcher did the strangest thing. With his nose to the ground and his tail wagging, he sniffed in a small circle. Suddenly he stopped, raised his head and barked excitedly. Then he put his nose to the ground again and, following his nose, ran right to the bush where she hid. When he saw her, he barked happily again and licked her chin.

"See?" said boy. "It's like hide-and-seek. Fetcher can find you by your smell. Good dog!" He patted his happy companion.

"That's all very clever," Girl grumbled, "but I don't see what *good* it is."

"You'll see. Everything Fetcher learns will come in handy one day."

The days continued to be hot and cloudless, as summers were in that part of the world. At sunrise, the small group would be ready for breakfast. During the hottest part of the afternoon, they sought out trees beneath which to rest and take lunch. Then they walked till sundown, always heading towards the hazy purple mountains that grew no larger.

They saw no sign of the merchant, and Girl often wondered if they would ever find Ramose and return the map, or if this wasn't just a good excuse for a lovely long walk. Sometimes she found herself feeling uneasy for a new reason. Until she met Boy, Girl had not realized that hers wasn't much of a name. Now she joined Boy in the desire for a *real* name.

One night while Boy and Mother slept, she sat looking at the moon and stars overhead, just as she had done in their little hut. The river has a name, she thought. It's called Euphrates. And I'll bet the city has a name, too. Mother calls me little fish, but that's not my name.

Then she curled up on her side and closed her eyes. Perhaps I'll find a name in the city. She yawned. Perhaps if I am patient, I, too, will earn a name.

But Boy was less patient. Finally he complained. "We've been travelling for days and days. When will we have an adventure? I'm bored!"

"You must wait," replied Mother calmly, "and you will see what you will see. That's what a Catswalk is."

But, secretly, Mother was worried because they were running out of food. She had brought enough for two and was now feeding twice that number. The good little goat still gave milk, for she ate plenty of grasses and bushes, but soon they might have to live on only her milk and whatever dates they found.

There came an evening when Mother prepared to serve the last barley cakes. Boy and Fetcher had gone off, as usual, to wherever they went when the group stopped. Then the bushes parted, and out stepped Boy with a great grin on his face. Fetcher, bounding at his heels, carried a fat duck.

"Good dog," said Boy. He took the duck from Fetcher's mouth and presented it to an astonished Mother. "Can you cook this for supper?"

Just in time, thought Mother, as she prepared the duck. In the time it takes to recite a riddle, she had it cleaned, plucked, and sizzling on a spit over the fire.

"Wherever . . . ?" began Girl.

"I knocked it out of the air with a stick," Boy explained, "and Fetcher caught the duck, almost in midair! I'm going to make a better stick for throwing." And he set to work whittling a big piece of wood while the delicious smell of roast duck filled the air.

The next day he and Fetcher brought back another duck, and the day after that they brought down a rabbit.

Poor thing, Girl thought, looking at the limp gray form in Fetcher's jaws, but at their evening meal she had to admit that it tasted very good. Thereafter, the little group ate meat every night.

Except for one particular night. Mother and the children were watching the evening's catch, a large duck, sizzle and brown over the fire. One moment Girl was thinking that she was glad it was a *big* duck, and the next moment a huge, tawny lioness ambled into the firelight!

Boy reached for his throwing stick, and Fetcher whined and growled. Girl tensed her body to run, but Mother put a reassuring paw on her arm. Slowly the gray cat rose, walked over, and stood before the immense beast. Girl caught her breath. Mother looked so small! She who was the last of the Great Cats stood like a kitten before the gilded paws of this animal.

Mother spoke in a language the children had never heard. "What is she saying?" asked Boy.

"Ssh!" Girl whispered. "I thinking she's speaking Lion."

And the lioness answered in the same language. Then Mother went back to the fire for the duck and placed it, along with some of the last goat cheese, in a basket. This she presented to the lioness.

Girl watched as the lioness ate, and tried not to hear the sounds her own empty stomach made. After all, she reasoned, it's better to have an empty stomach than to fill a lion's stomach.

The great animal finished half the duck and raised her head to look at Mother. Then, as the children watched wistfully—half a meal would have been nice, too, thought Girl—Mother wrapped the leavings neatly in her own shawl and presented them to the uninvited guest. The lioness took the package in her mouth, growled politely, and stalked off into the darkness.

"Remember," Mother told the children, who were staring after the departing beast, "she has young ones to feed."

The travellers ate dates and the rest of the goat cheese before going to sleep. As was now her habit, Girl unrolled the map and studied it by firelight. She had a feeling about what she would find, and—yes! Over the little group of trees that represented the oasis where they slept: HERE THERE BE LIONS.

Mother was already asleep, purring in her dreams. Girl snuggled up to the soft fur, wondering if she would ever be able to read about things *before* they happened.

The next morning the troop continued on their way along the footpath. Where the path made a slight bend to follow the river, they came upon something lying on the ground. Mother picked it up. Her shawl! She shook it out and examined it critically. "Just a few grease spots. I can wash those out in the river."

And after that, they were never again bothered by lions.

It got so that Girl felt she'd rather be bothered by lions than by Boy. He was becoming such a pest! One minute he would be a fine friend and help her pick green herbs for Mother by the riverside. Then he'd spy a disgusting grub in the ground and wave it in front of her face.

"Yum, yum!" he would tease. "I bet it's delicious!"

Girl would sigh impatiently, "Oh, Boy, you're such a baby," and turn to pick more plants.

Then Boy would do something especially awful, like put the nasty thing down the back of her dress. He would laugh and laugh, as though he had just done the funniest thing.

Honestly, Girl thought, he has developed a most obnoxious sense of humor. She sought out the company of Mother more often. Mother understood and told her, "Don't worry, little fish. He'll grow out of it."

Girl preferred to spend more time with her map, anyway. Trying to read it had become a wonderful game. Sometimes it seemed that she could almost make out a word here and there. Finally she found that she could read something new, and something that lay *ahead*, rather than behind them! On the map, on the path next to the river, was a big square. And over it, in tiny letters, she read: KISH.

So that was the city's name.

THE DAY AFTER GIRL DISCOVERED THE CITY'S NAME

she spied something on the horizon. Far in the distance, next to the winding river that shimmered in the noonday heat, stood a vast blue shape; around it, the flat plain unfolded for many miles. And way beyond the plain, still hazy and purple, lay the mountains. Could this strange shape be Kish she asked Boy.

"Yes," Boy informed her. "But it's not the city I came from. Mine is called Erech. I didn't know there was another city until I looked at your map. I thought mine was the only one in the world."

"Silly boy," said Mother, with an impatient twitch of her tail. "What do you know? There are many cities."

Girl was shocked at the way Mother spoke. She had never before heard the gray cat be rude. That night she took out the map again and looked for the city. There was the word, but it seemed to have grown bigger. Carefully she read it: KISH.

Each day the city appeared larger as they approached it. Girl asked Mother a thousand questions about this fabled place, but Mother only acted annoyed.

"I don't like cities," she told Girl.

"But we *must* go to the city, to find Ramose," reasoned Girl. "Mustn't we?"

Mother sighed. "Of course. But," she added, "I don't like cities."

Boy said, "I'm not afraid of cities. I'll take care of you."

"I'm not afraid," Mother snapped. "I just don't like cities."

One evening the travellers approached a small oasis to find rest for the night. A group of men were already gathered under the trees. They had pulled their carts into a semicircle, and their unhitched oxen grazed on the small patches of grass nearby. They were a caravan of merchants, their carts laden with trade goods from Kish.

The caravan leader was a fat, friendly man, his beard streaked with gray. His fleecy cloak of sheep's wool covered shoulders tanned like leather by the sun. He bade the cat and the children welcome and invited them to share his food and fire that night—an invitation they gratefully accepted. Mother was quite happy to taste someone else's cooking for a change, and Boy was growing weary of hunting every night.

Soon Boy and Girl sat at the leader's feet while he entertained them with tales of his travels. "I've been to every land in the world, young miss," he boasted to Girl. "What would you like to hear about? The land of sands and solemn god-kings? The place where folk have hair the color of the sun and eyes like the sky, yet live in caves and know no writing? Or the vast green jungles wherein dwell a people, black as night, among savage beasts?"

"Oh, please," begged Girl, "tell me about Kish."

"Oho! I can show you what I brought from Kish, for the trade was good." He strode over to his wagon with the children close at his heels. "Have you ever seen such as this?" He smiled. They stood on tiptoe and peered inside.

"Ah!" was all Girl could say. Not even Ramose's pack had contained such an array of rainbow-hued fabrics, ivory and tortoise shell combs, beads, bracelets, and rings. The caravan leader handed her a long-handled object with a shiny silver surface. She looked into it and saw a girl staring back at her through startled dark eyes.

"Ah!" again. She dropped the thing, and the fat, laughing man caught it as it fell. She pointed to it. "Who is that?"

The caravan leader was still chuckling. "This is called a mirror. The girl you saw is yourself." He handed her a tiny pot of green paint and showed her how to smear the paint on her eyelids.

Why, thought Girl, looking in the mirror, now my eyes look like Mother's. Later, she wanted to wear the paint on her eyelids while she slept, but Mother wouldn't let her.

"Young girls need to keep their faces clean," she declared, and licked the paint right off with her rough, pink tongue. She was still in a bad mood. "I don't like cities."

This time, when Girl checked the map before going to sleep, she found the words had changed. Now she read: KISH. BE CAREFUL.

Girl lay back and thought about this warning. The camp was quiet. On the other side of the dying campfire, the merchant grunted now and then in his sleep. Mother doesn't like cities, she thought drowsily, and the map tells me to be careful. But Boy will take care of us; he promised.

In the morning, Mother and the children bade the caravan good-bye, and by midafternoon they reached the shadow of the city's great walls. The narrow footpath leading to Kish had widened and was now a vast stone-paved road. Caravans and foot travellers passed through massive wooden gates that were set in the ten-foot-thick mud-brick walls.

And here it was that Mother sat down and flatly refused to go any farther. "I don't like cities," she said once more. "I must wait for you here." She led the little goat to a small clump of trees that grew right outside the wall. "You go. I'll stay with the goat."

But as Girl walked off with Boy and Fetcher, Mother called after her, "Little fish, be careful!"

Just like the map, thought Girl.

They joined the stream of people entering the gates of Kish. On either side of the heavy gates stood an immense statue of a winged bull with a man's head.

The bearded stone face smiled down cruelly at Girl as she passed. And then, suddenly, they were in the city!

It was festival time, and the crowds surrounding them, mostly farmers and merchants, had come to buy and sell at the bazaar. As they set out their wares, the merchants jostled the two children and their dog impatiently. Girl had to duck out of the way as a chariot passed, almost on top of her. Fetcher barked angrily at the departing wheels, but it was so crowded the driver had not even seen her.

There was too much to look at all at once. As far as Girl could see were rows of square, windowless, mud-brick houses. The narrow, dusty streets that wound between them were crowded with laughing, chattering people. Everywhere merchants had spread wares on mats and rugs, under striped awnings, and in wooden stalls. The ornately dressed throng passed among the displays, inspecting merchandise while they nibbled tiny delicious-smelling sausages. Women with elaborately curled hair and eyebrows pencilled in darkly held enamelled earrings to their ears and studied the results in polished silver mirrors. The men's beards were curled and perfumed. And everyone wore colorful, fringed garments.

Suddenly Girl was acutely aware of her own simple dress of undyed goat's fleece. She forgot her beautiful rainbow sash and thought only of the splendor surrounding her. Two teenaged girls strolled by, followed by a servant who held a parasol over their heads to protect them from the sun. Both girls wore golden headdresses in the shape of leaves and flowers. They glanced at Girl and turned away, giggling and whispering to each other. Were they laughing at her? Girl felt her cheeks grow hot with shame.

But Boy clenched his fist angrily, and he threw his cloak around her shoulders to hide her worn garment. Girl pulled the cloak around her tightly and gave Boy a grateful smile. Then she turned her attention to the merchants and their wares and soon became so engrossed in the dazzling array of wonders offered for sale that she forgot the people around her.

As she passed from one stall to the next, Girl failed to notice that she and Boy had become separated by the milling crowd. Examining the brass pots that filled a mat, each one so highly polished that it reflected her face like a mirror,

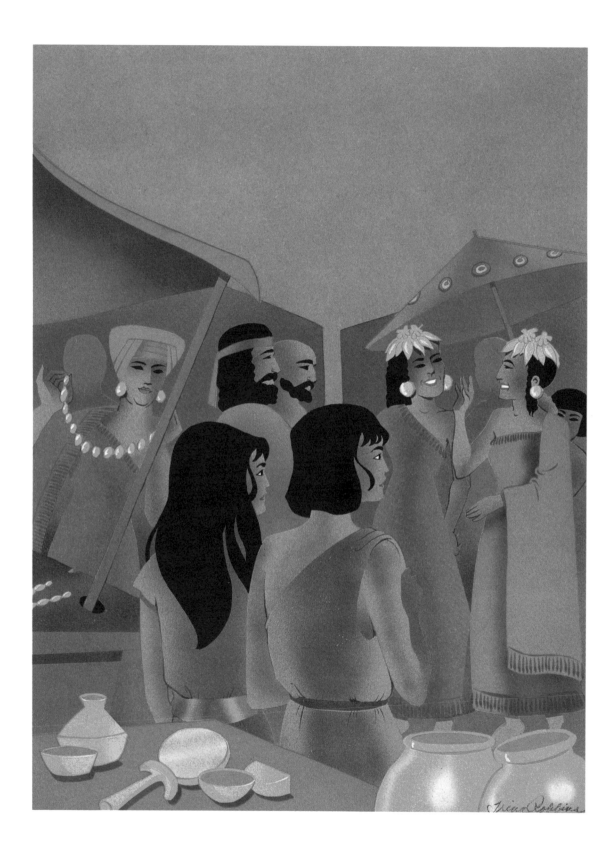

Girl thought fleetingly that Mother would like one. But when she turned her attention to the ornate sandals displayed in the next stall, she forgot even Mother who waited outside the city gates. How lovely the sandals were! The toes came to a point and curled up. Flowers and scrollwork had been carved into the leather and filled in with many colors. Beads had even been sewn into some pairs. Girl looked down self-consciously at her own bare brown feet. How could she ever wear anything as dainty as those sandals?

She passed from stall to dizzying stall, her senses drinking in all that was offered. The air was heavy with the combined smell of incense and barbecued meats. Here a man juggled scarlet pomegranates, there one played a silver flute while a woman—her hair pulled into one long braid that ended in a golden bell—danced, tinkling in time to the music. Here were brightly hued garments, which dripped with row upon row of deep fringes, like those worn by the folk surrounding her. She saw blue, beaded collars, like the one Ramose had worn. Could Ramose be here? She scanned the marketplace, but her eye was distracted again by colors that shone in the sun.

Entranced, Girl danced over to the source of the colors and found a table covered with bangles, each enamelled a different color.

"You like them?" asked the merchant. "Hold out your arm."

And he covered Girl's outstretched arm with bracelets, putting them on so they progressed from green to blue to purple to red to orange and, finally, to yellow. Now she truly wore a rainbow.

Girl gave a gleeful shriek. "They're beautiful! Are they for me?"

"Yes," responded the merchant, "if you can pay for them."

Girl's face fell. Of course! She saw that all around her people were exchanging gold and silver coins for the goods. "But I have nothing to give you," she faltered.

"Yes you do," answered the merchant, and he reached for Girl's amulet. "This will do nicely."

At first Girl backed away. Mother had picked out the amber carving especially for her, and she shouldn't part with it. But she looked again at the jingling rainbow on her arm. Resolutely, she pulled the chain from around her

neck and held it out to the merchant. He snatched it greedily, and Girl knew at once she shouldn't have given away the jewel.

Where were Boy and Fetcher? Girl spun around, desperately seeking a glimpse of them, but her vision was obscured by the jostling shoppers and her eyes were dazzled by their riotous colors. She looked for the big gate through which the three had come but couldn't find it. After wandering the mazelike streets, she had lost all sense of direction.

Her uneasiness turned to panic. "Boy! Fetcher!" Tears started from her eyes. The music and laughter and calls from the merchants were so loud that even if Boy had been near, he would not have heard her anxious voice.

Girl ran through the narrow, winding streets, sometimes bumping into people who pushed her away with impatient oaths, calling for Boy and Fetcher.

Soon she found herself in a different neighborhood. The rows of houses had thinned out, and she stood alone in a paved square. Towering over her from each of the four corners was a massive statue of a muscular man with the head of a lion. In the square's center rose the biggest building Girl had ever seen. At the very top of the steps, which seemed to climb to the sky, sat a temple, its walls covered with a shiny mosaic of red and blue tile.

Now she knew she was completely lost. Weary and weeping with vexation and dismay, she collapsed upon the marble steps.

CAN THIS BE AN OFFERING, PLACED ON THE TEMPLE STEPS?"
The gentle voice startled Girl; she looked up. A man in long purple robes smiled down at her. His head was shaved, like Ramose, but he was one of Girl's people, tall and stocky. His skin was uncommonly pale, as though he spent most of his time out of the ever-present sun.

"Why, it's a living girl!" he exclaimed happily. "And beautiful as a dream. Are you lost and frightened, little one? Let me help you find a happier place." And he held out his hand.

He beamed serenely, and Girl felt she could trust him. She sniffed, wiping her cheeks with a grubby fist, and took his hand. Perhaps he would help her find Boy and Fetcher. He led her up the steps and into the temple.

The interior was so dark that at first Girl couldn't see a thing. As her eyes adjusted to the darkness, she saw that oil lamps were lit, and after a while she could see quite well by the tiny flickering flames they produced. The air smelled thick and sweet from the incense that smoked in brass dishes. The vast, pillared room was filled with soft couches, and in the half-light, she could make out sleeping figures.

The purple-robed man laid a gentle hand upon her shoulder. "These are the dreamers, child, and I am their priest." Waving his hand, he indicated the couch-filled room. "We have forsaken the sorrow of the harsh world outside and lie here dreaming of better lands. Many have even forsaken their families."

Girl felt uneasy at the thought that men and women would desert their loved ones for dreams, and she decided this was not a place she wanted to be. But she was so tired—or was it the incense making her groggy? The heavy scent seemed to draw away her energy.

I want to take a nice, long nap, she thought, and when I wake up, I can worry about . . . Who was she supposed to worry about? A boy and a dog came to mind, and a large gray cat, but she couldn't quite remember who they were.

The priest scooped her up and held her before the dozing worshippers. Some of them stirred and looked up at her.

"Look," he announced. "Our dreams have sent us a girl. Isn't she pretty? We'll dress her up and keep her. She can join us in our dreams."

The sweet smoke numbed Girl's mind. Was she already dreaming, or did the priest wipe her tear-stained face gently with a scented cloth? Did he really cover her simple shift with a silken robe of deepest purple, place glittering rings upon her fingers, set a silver circlet around her hair?

In her half-dream, he placed her on a cloud-soft couch. She sank into the deep cushions with a luxurious sigh. Never had she felt so tired, never had she felt so comfortable!

As Girl dozed, she seemed to drift upon the perfumed smoke as it wafted out of the temple. Down the steps she soared, and then rode a breeze through the streets and out of the great gates of Kish.

How easy it is now to leave the city, she thought drowsily.

The breeze became a wind, speeding her across the dusty plain and high in the air, until she was level with the mountains, which now loomed before her—the very same mountains Girl had always seen from her home. She willed herself to float towards them.

The mountains rose to jagged peaks, and Girl drifted towards the highest pinnacle. Soon she saw that what she had taken to be a mountaintop was a tall castle, built upon the rocky summit. She flew through an open door. Inside, the hallways were dark and deserted. More light, thought Girl, and instantly torches, set in sconces along the stone walls, flared to life.

That's better, she thought, and never touched the wooden floor as she drifted down the hall. She willed herself through an arched doorway into a vast,

empty room. Marble pillars supported a beamed ceiling, and at one end stood a throne of carven cedar, inlaid with mother-of-pearl.

Of course, Girl realized, that's my throne. Regally, she sank into it, thinking, what a pleasant dream! But there should be people here, she decided. Instantly the room filled with her adoring subjects.

Across the room a large window let in the sunlight, and through it she saw violet mountains swoop down to meet the rolling sea. A small gray cat sat on the windowsill, gazing at her with calm green eyes.

Girl faltered. There's something about a cat, she told herself, that I should remember. But I can't!

She rose from her throne and glided across to where the cat perched. The small animal jumped gracefully and disappeared out the window. Girl followed closely. But the cat was nowhere to be seen, and Girl fell, unafraid, through the sky and into the night-blue ocean with a great splash.

Down she sank, startling schools of rainbow-colored fish, and the water grew darker and colder. Then her feet touched bottom, and she stood on the ocean floor! Around her, the darkness lifted and was replaced by a faint glow.

The light came from scores of phosphorescent fish, gleaming blue and green as they swam about Girl. She followed them, delighted, to a wrecked ship, which sprawled on the ocean floor like a dead whale. They swam through holes in the rotting hull into a cabin where, to Girl's horror, skeletons seemed to dance in the water. But they were only swaying with the currents, and the brilliant fish swam playfully through the ribs and eye sockets. Girl shivered in the icy water and willed her dream to take on a more pleasant tone.

In one corner of the cabin, strange children played catch with the glittering treasure that spilled from a great wooden chest. From their hips down, the children had long, scaly fish tails. The merchildren waved for her to join them. One tossed Girl a giant pearl, big as an apricot. Laughing, she tossed it back. Another threw a gold coin, which Girl caught easily. At that moment, a beam of sunlight penetrated the murky waters and bounced off the coin. How lovely! She had forgotten about the sun.

Suddenly, Girl became aware of the intense cold, so, with her face raised to the light, she followed the beam to the ocean's surface. Girl rose up out of the

water and continued to rise towards the sun. She passed through the blue sky and then floated free in the darker deep space. The sun became just one of the millions of twinkling stars, which glittered—blue, scarlet, and gold—like jewels from the treasure she had left behind. Fascinated, Girl gathered up handfuls of stars, tossed them into the blackness, and watched them fall, leaving glowing trails.

Then, twisting around in the dark sky, she followed the falling stars headfirst, back down to the revolving green ball, which was the earth. As she approached it, she could make out the brown plain and the fertile green strip alongside the river. Soon she could see the walled city of Kish and the tiny figure of Mother, who waited at the city gates. The figure grew in size as Girl got closer. Soon she could see Mother's face. And Mother was looking right at her!

The Great Cat appeared reproachful. "This is how they sacrifice to their god," Mother explained. "They find a beautiful, innocent child to introduce to the dreams. The child cannot stop dreaming and soon dreams itself to death! You never should have traded away the amulet."

Girl jerked awake with a scream. She was sitting upright on the couch. Silence and the even breathing of sleepers surrounded her. The room was stifling. She dared not breathe any more of the poisonous fumes, but she could not hold her breath. Fighting the grogginess that invaded her head, she stumbled outside into the fresh air.

GIRL LEANED AGAINST A MARBLE PILLAR, GRATEFULLY gasping in lungfuls of air. She shook her head, and the cobwebs inside dispersed. But how long have I been dreaming? She wondered, has it been hours? Days? *Years*?

Out of the corner of her eye, Girl noticed something brown wedged between the pillar and the temple steps. She pulled it out. Boy's cloak, still lying where she discarded it carelessly—how long ago? She hugged it to her chest, trying to fight back tears, and sat on the bottom step, feeling lost and very alone.

All of a sudden, Girl's leg felt wet and cold. She looked down. Fetcher was licking it! "Am I glad to see you!"

Fetcher, his fine brown fur hopelessly tangled, his tail full of burrs, barked eagerly, happy to see a friend, and put his dusty paws on Girl's lap. She scratched behind his ears, which started his tail wagging.

"Fetcher! Where's Boy?"

Fetcher whined sadly at the mention of his friend.

"Come on! Where's Boy?" But the dog didn't know.

Then Girl remembered the cloak. Would Boy's scent still be on it? Would Fetcher really be able to find him, just by smelling the cloak? She held it out, and the eager dog snuffled.

"Go, Fetcher," she yelled. "Go find Boy!"

Fetcher snuffled and snaffled at the piece of cloth, sniffled once more, whined and gave a little yip. Then he ran in a circle with his nose to the ground. Finally he raised his head, howled once, and loped down the street, tail wagging. Girl followed him, running to keep up. Every now and then Fetcher paused to sniff the ground again and repeated the process of running in a little circle until he picked up the scent anew. Then he would be off in a new direction, with Girl racing close behind.

They continued on in this fashion until they found their path blocked by a tall wall of mud bricks and a thick wooden gate. Fetcher barked loudly and angrily. His friend was somewhere on the other side of the wall! He tried unsuccessfully to leap over it and barked some more.

Girl looked about for help, but they had come far from the bazaar and the streets were deserted. I suppose, she reasoned, that I'll have to climb over it.

"You wait here," she commanded, raising her voice to be heard over the dog's frenzied barking. "I'll come back with Boy. I promise."

She surveyed the wall. It reached up several feet over her head but was not too high to climb, or to jump from once she got to the top. She started climbing, fitting her bare toes into the open spaces between bricks.

She was not more than a quarter of the way up when a rough voice shouted, "Ho! Get away from there!"

Strong hands grabbed Girl's shoulders, pulled her off the wall, and placed her back on the ground firmly. She found herself staring up at a huge, black-bearded man, who stared back at her from under bushy brows with eyes that held just a hint of amusement. A dagger hung from the belt of his leather uniform. Fetcher growled at the man's heels. Girl tried not to appear frightened, but the fierce-looking stranger noticed her fear and knelt down so he was closer to her height.

"This is the palace of Ur-Zababa, the Black Lord of Kish," he explained gently. "I am the guardian of the gate, and young girls are not welcome here."

Though Girl was close to tears, she put on her bravest face. "We're looking for our friend," she protested, "and his trail has led us here. Have you seen a boy with tangled black hair that goes past his ears? He's a bit taller than me, and probably pretty dirty."

"Ah, the hungry boy!" he chuckled. "Better give up on that one, for you'll not see him again."

"But why not? Where is he?"

"That one is locked away in the deepest dungeon, and very sorry now that he ate what he shouldn't have."

Girl's heart sank. "What do you mean?" she faltered.

"Well then," began the guard, "let me tell you what happened. . . . One fine day," he continued, "His Blackness decided to parade through the streets of Kish, so his subjects could see his magnificence. Unfortunately, when Ur-Zababa promenades the streets, all his subjects must fall upon their faces before him, so they don't really get to see him anyway.

"So His Blackness was parading through Kish, and all his subjects were lying flat upon their faces, when up strides this scruffy boy, bold as you please. He marched right up to Ur-Zababa and asked for a position in the palace, as though he were seeking employment from some ordinary merchant. 'I have come to earn my name,' he announced brazenly.

"The royal guards were astounded at his audacity. 'Shall we kill him now, Sire, or later?' they asked.

"But, wouldn't you know it, the Black Lord was delighted by the bold lad! 'You are a fine, brave boy,' he told the young one. 'You shall be my pet and sit next to me at table. And if you keep me amused, perhaps I will give you a name.'

"The great Black Lord took the boy by his grubby hand and led him through the palace gates—I myself held the gates open for them!—and into the palace. He took the boy to the banquet hall, where sat fine ladies and gentlemen of the court, gossiping as they sipped wine from silver goblets. There, as slaves waved great plumed fans, he gave the boy a seat next to his own at the long table.

"Trained monkeys in golden vests set the table with fruits and meats and sweets. In front of the Black Lord they placed a tray piled high with round golden fruits.

"Well, young lady, I hope you have better manners than that boy, because without ever a 'please' or a 'may I,' he plucked one of the shining spheres from

the tray and bit into it. He so savored the juicy pulp that at first he didn't notice a terrible hush had fallen over the Black Lord's company. Then he looked about and noticed that everyone at the table had stopped whatever they were doing to stare, with wide eyes and open mouths. A grim-faced guard strode over, picked him up by the scruff of his neck, and shook him soundly.

"The Black Lord frowned. 'Now you've done it. The golden fruit is forbidden to all but the Black Lord himself. I suppose you'll have to be punished.' His Blackness sighed. 'To the dungeons with him.'

"And the wretched boy was dragged off by his long, tangled black hair."

"And that," finished the guardian of the gate, "was that."

Girl was horrified. "But when will they let him out?"

"I imagine," replied the guardian, "about a week after he dies. Then they'll drag the body out and throw it onto the offal heap." And the big man laughed at his witty answer until he coughed.

Girl started to turn away. Boy was finished; nothing she could do would help him. She would never see him again.

After all, she told herself, it serves him right. Mother *did* try to teach him manners, but he just wouldn't listen. And, even if I *could* get him out, he wouldn't thank me. He'd probably just tease me, or drop a slug down the neck of my dress. Stupid Boy!

Then she remembered how Boy had thrown his cloak over her when she was embarrassed about her ragged dress. Fetcher began to whine, and she looked down into his round eyes. She squared her shoulders and faced the guard.

"I must speak with the Black Lord."

"Now, now. A nice thing like you doesn't want to go in *there*," began the guardian. But then he saw Girl's resolute expression and knew there would be no dissuading her.

"Very well. But you must pay for an audience with His Blackness, you know. Now, that circlet on your forehead looks to be silver . . ." and he reached for the circlet.

But Fetcher bared his teeth at the man and snarled menacingly. The guardian of the gate backed away. "Well, I won't take it from you. But still," he insisted, "you must give it to me or I can't let you pass."

Girl didn't hesitate for a moment. She removed the circlet from around her head and handed it to him. He pushed on the gates and they swung open slowly. Fetcher sprang forward eagerly.

"No, Fetcher," commanded Girl, "you must stay here. You wait for me, and I'll be back with Boy."

Fetcher whined in protest but lay down obediently to wait in front of the wall. Passing through the gate, Girl noticed that without the weight of the circlet on her brow, she could hold her head higher. A long path of dark flagstones led to the palace, which was an immense, low building constructed entirely of black stone. On either side of the path, where flower gardens should have been, were chunks of granite and sand, dotted with an occasional, round white stone. With a sudden thrill of horror, Girl realized that the white stones were human skulls! She shuddered and turned away, trying not to look down until she reached an ornately carved ebony door.

Immediately, two spears crossed in the air before her, barring her way. The two uniformed guards who held the spears stood on either side of the door. Girl had thought the guardian of the gate was big, but these two were even bigger.

They spoke as one. "Halt! None can enter into the presence of Ur-Zababa, ruler of these lands."

"I can, too, enter," protested Girl hotly. "The guardian of the gate gave me permission in exchange for my silver circlet . . ." And she realized immediately she had said too much, for at the mention of the silver circlet, greed appeared in the guards' faces.

"And what will you offer us," inquired the first guard, "to let you into the palace?"

"Look, Humbaba!" exclaimed the second guard. "Look at her hands! She has three rings on each."

Humbaba grabbed Girl's trembling hand and looked at the rings that had been placed there by the priest in the temple of dreamers. "One gold, one silver, and one copper, and the same on the other hand."

"Don't be frightened, little miss," the second guard told her. "After all, I have a daughter of my own, I do."

Humbaba nodded. "We'll just take the gold rings, one ring each, and you may keep the silver and the copper."

Willingly, Girl drew the gold rings off her shaking fingers and handed them to the guards who opened the heavy black door obligingly. "You may enter the palace," they announced in unison.

As she passed inside, Humbaba warned, "Careful now, there's a step."

And, indeed, there was a step down. Girl found herself following a dimly lit corridor that sloped down gently. She was sorry to hear the big door close behind her, for now she was completely alone. There was no sound other than her own hushed footsteps and no direction other than downwards. Finally she came to a place where the corridor branched. Which way to go?

Two more guards stood at attention in the intersection of the two corridors. She approached them. "Please, sirs, which way is the throne room?"

The guards smiled at each other. "And why would a little thing like yourself be looking for the throne room?" asked one. "Didn't your mother teach you to stay out of trouble?"

Girl drew herself up so she was standing as straight as she could. "I have permission to see the Black Lord," she insisted, "from the guardian of the gate, and from the guards at the palace door."

"And why should we let you pass? What will you give us if we show you the way?" smiled one of the guards.

This time Girl was prepared. "I will give you each a silver ring." She drew off the silver rings and handed them to the guards.

"Well now," said the first, "that'll do fine. The throne room is this way." And pointing with his thumb, he indicated the corridor to the left.

40

As Girl walked on, he called after her, "You be careful! The Black Lord is a tricky one, and if he takes a liking to you, it may be worse than if he doesn't like you at all."

The guards laughed as Girl continued on. The passageway through which Girl walked still sloped steadily downhill, and she knew she was quite a ways underground. The air felt cool and smelled faintly of moist earth, and the stone floor was chilly beneath her bare feet. Please, she prayed silently, no more guards.

The corridor branched off once more, and Girl turned into the branch on her right but saw quickly that after several feet it ended abruptly in a stone wall. She retraced her steps and started down the other corridor, encountering another guard immediately.

At least there's only one this time, she thought gratefully.

The guard snapped to attention and drew his spear. "Halt! What do I see here? A child in the halls of the Black Lord's palace? How came you here?"

Girl sighed, hoping desperately that this was the last guard she would meet. "I crave an audience with the Black Lord," she began patiently. "I have permission from the guardian of the gate, the guards of the palace door, the guards of the corridor . . ."

"Never mind that," he snapped, "what will you give me?"

She held out her hands.

"Humph! Only copper. But I'll take them both."

Quickly, she stripped the last rings off her fingers and tossed them to the now-smiling guard. "You may pass," he told her.

About twenty feet past the guard, the corridor ended in a curtain of black velvet, which was covered with embroidery of silver moons and stars. This must be the entrance to the throne room! Girl ran towards it, but yet another guard stepped forward, seemingly out of nowhere, to block her path.

"Who dares," he bellowed, "attempt to enter into the audience of the great Black Lord unannounced?"

Girl nearly wept with frustration. "I suppose I must pay to be announced," she guessed bitterly.

"Of course."

Girl still wore the rainbow-colored bangles for which she had bartered her amulet. She pulled them off and held them out to the guard.

He drew back, looking deeply offended. "I don't want those," he sniffed. "They're worthless junk."

Girl despaired. She had nothing else to offer, and she was so close to the Black Lord!

"Ah, but this pretty thing, now," the guard fingered the hem of her purple robe, "feels like it might be pure silk. Worth quite a bit, I'll wager."

Without another word, Girl pulled the garment over her head. Beneath it she still wore her white homespun dress with the rainbow sash knotted at her waist.

"You wait here," the guard told her, and he disappeared behind the velvet hanging. Girl heard him shout, "A young lady craves audience with your Royal Blackness."

A deep voice replied, "Bid her enter," and at these words the guard pulled back the drapery.

"Go on," he whispered, then nudged her forward. Shivering in the chill air, but with her head high, Girl entered the throne room.

THE THRONE ROOM WAS IMMENSE AND SILENT. NO SOUND echoed among the pillars of onyx and black marble save the chittering of monkeys in golden vests, who scampered along the floor or clung to the tops of pillars. On the other side of the cavernous room, draped in black robes embroidered with golden stars, Ur-Zababa sat, slumped on a squat, onyx throne. Even at that distance Girl saw his piercing eyes, which studied her from beneath thick, black brows that joined over his hooked nose. Before him lay the members of his court, flat upon their faces.

A small black cat picked its way delicately and disdainfully among the prone subjects. Girl's heart leaped with joy at the sight of it, but when it turned its head to look at her, she saw no intelligence in its eyes.

It's only a lesser cat, she realized, disappointed, and cannot speak, poor thing. Still, it is every bit as beautiful as Mother.

The thought of Mother gave her confidence until the Black Lord crooked one fat, beringed finger and beckoned silently for her to approach. Girl's first reaction was to turn and run all the way back from whence she had come. But, slowly, she steadied herself and approached the throne, threading her way between the flattened worshippers.

He likes people who aren't afraid of him, she reminded herself. She stopped directly in front of the throne, made a respectful curtsy, and waited.

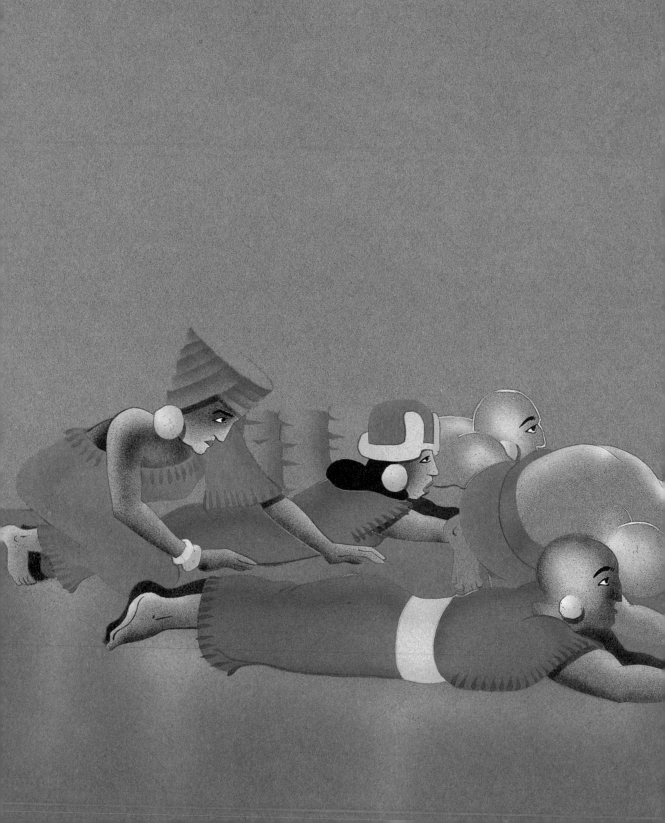

The Black Lord stroked his black, curled beard and regarded her in silence solemnly. Finally he spoke. "What?" he exclaimed fiercely. "No paint upon your eyelids for an audience with the great Black Lord? No precious oils, no perfumes? Hair all uncurled?

"No jewelry?" he roared. "No fine silken robes?"

Members of the court raised their heads to stare at the audacious child. Some of the women tittered. Girl tried not to cry but felt at least one tear escape and trickle down her cheek.

Suddenly, the Black Lord's lips drew back, revealing clenched white teeth.

Why, he's smiling! Girl realized.

"I like it," he announced, looking around at his court. "So plain, so simple, so charming and unspoiled."

Surreptitiously, several of the women slipped off their rings and bracelets and hid them in folds of their garments.

He turned back to Girl. "So," he continued, "what does your charmingness and simpleness want with my Blackness and Greatness?"

Girl gazed up earnestly at the fierce ruler. Did she detect genuine merriment in those deep-set eyes? Her voice emerged as a frightened whisper. "Please, your Great Blackness, I wish the freedom of the boy whom you have locked in your deepest dungeon."

The twinkle left the black eyes. The man on the throne scowled, and his face darkened. "That wretched boy, he went and spoiled my fun!" Even the monkeys stopped their chatter. All eyes were upon the girl and the great ruler.

"I rather enjoyed the cheeky little thing," he continued in a more reasonable tone. "I get so tired of my squirmy subjects. 'Yes, your Blackness' and 'No, your Blackness,' that's all they ever say. But that boy was different. He wasn't at all afraid of me! We could have had such good times together."

The dark ruler scowled again. "Then he had to go and spoil it by eating the golden fruit, which only a king such as I may eat." He shrugged a lordly shrug. "What else could I do? He ate what he shouldn't have, and now he must rot in my deepest dungeon, supplementing his meager diet of raw onions with rats and bugs."

The Black Lord leaned closer to Girl and whispered. "If only he had waited until we were alone, I might have let him get away with it. But once everyone had seen what he had done—well, rules are rules."

He gazed at her with renewed interest. "But you are a brave and amusing child," he murmured. "I think I will make you my new pet. There'll be no golden fruit for you, either, but all the meats and sweets you desire. Around your neck you will wear a golden collar with a gold chain attached to the wall so that you cannot escape.

"But, of course, you will not want to escape. I shall lead you around by your golden chain, and you will say clever things. We will watch executions together. It will be such fun!"

The prospect of becoming the Black Lord's pet seemed downright dismal. "Your Blackness," she began again, hoping not to hurt his feelings, "flattered as I am by your generous offer, I have a mother waiting for me outside the city gates . . ."

"A mother!" The dark ruler snorted. "No mother is as important as my royal Blackness! Let your mother wait forever.

"Anyway," he added petulantly, "I need to be amused. I'm bored."

Desperately, Girl cast about in her mind for some way to distract the fearsome man on the black throne. How to free Boy from his deep, deep prison and stay free myself? That's a riddle.

A riddle! Girl brightened. She had a plan, but did she dare . . . ?

"Oh Great One, do you like riddles?"

The Black Lord grinned, showing his sharp, white teeth again. "I love riddles! But it gets annoying. My subjects are afraid to ask me hard ones. They fear that if I can't guess the answer, I'll get angry and have them executed. Of course, they're right. . . . Do *you* know any riddles? Any hard ones?"

"Oh Great One, I propose a riddle contest."

"*You* propose?" The Black Lord drew himself up and peered down his hooked nose. "You presume!" And all the court, still lying flat on their stomachs, waited for him to summon the executioner. But instead he added mildly, "Go on. You interest me."

"I propose that if I can guess your riddles and you cannot guess mine, you will let me take the boy and leave the palace."

"Agreed. But if you lose," the ruler told her, "you must become my new pet, and the wretched boy will molder away deep below the ground."

THE FIRST RIDDLES GIRL AND UR-ZABABA EXCHANGED
were answered easily. She remembered Mother telling them on many a night, sitting before their cheery fire back in the little hut.

"What can you keep," asked the Black Lord, "even after giving it to someone else?"

"Not hard to answer," replied Girl. "My word. Now, tell me what has a mouth but never eats, a bed but never sleeps?"

The Black Lord yawned. "A river. These are too easy," he complained. "Here's a harder one: I pass before the sun without casting a shadow. What am I?"

Girl hesitated. She had never heard that one. Thinking of the terrible fate awaiting her and Boy if she guessed wrong didn't make things any easier. At that moment, the black velvet hangings which curtained the walls of the throne room blew open.

Of course! Girl thought. "You are the wind."

The Black Lord scowled. "I had not expected you to know that one. You are a smart girl. Take care that you do not act *too* smart."

Now it was Girl's turn. She thought about Mother and asked, "What is a cat and not a cat, and yet is a cat?"

"Easy to answer," grinned the Black Lord. "A kitten! You'll have to do better than that if you want to free the boy." Then he offered the hardest riddle yet. "It is so brittle," he said, "that to name it is to break it."

Girl frowned. What was the most delicate thing she knew? Glass? But you couldn't break glass just by naming it.

The great room was still. All the courtiers looked up, hardly breathing, awaiting her reply. A loud *Miaow* from the beautiful but lesser cat, who now sat in the center of the room, broke the hush.

And, suddenly, Girl knew the answer. "It is silence!" she announced triumphantly.

The Black Lord muttered, "You had help on that one, I think."

Girl smiled gratefully at the lesser cat, and for one moment it seemed that the eyes gleaming back at her were Mother's. But the gleam faded and left only the lesser cat, who yawned and went to sleep.

Clearly, Ur-Zababa was becoming impatient. "I grow weary, little one," he announced with a cruel smile. "You have one more chance to confound the great Black Lord, ruler of all about him. And after failing that, I must declare the game over and myself the winner."

Girl panicked. How can I possibly think of a riddle he doesn't know, she thought, when he is the all-powerful, all-frightening Black Lord, ruler of just about everything, and I'm only a girl who doesn't even have a proper name?

And she thought aloud, "What is my name?"

The Black Lord's eyebrows rose. He leaned forward on his throne with renewed interest. "That's an odd riddle. I must have three guesses to answer it, because I am the Black Lord."

Girl only nodded, scarcely trusting herself to speak.

The Black Lord made a steeple of his fingers and rested his chin upon them as he considered this. Finally he said, "Every third girl born in Kish is named Myrtle-by-the-Stream. It is by far the most fashionable name. So there is one chance in three that your name is Myrtle-by-the-Stream. Am I right?"

"Oh Great One," Girl responded nervously, "you are wrong." She held her breath as he guessed again.

"Perhaps you were named for the way you look—that is often done in this city. You probably didn't have that long black hair when you were a baby, but you must have been born with those big eyes that are the color of the sky at night. So my guess is that your name is Midnight Sky."

Girl found her voice. "I am sorry, my lord, but you are wrong again."

The Black Lord's brows lowered, and he glared down at her from his black throne. He had never failed at a riddle game before.

He guessed once more. "It's not so hard," he bluffed. "Your mother probably waited till you were grown a bit to see what kind of girl you would become before she named you. And you became a courageous little thing, to challenge the Black Lord himself. Like a tiny bee, you are, who stings the all-powerful. That is what your mother named you: Honey Bee."

Girl let out a deep breath and shook her head. The Black Lord had lost! His great hands knotted into fists, and veins stood out on his forehead. Seeing this, the courtiers ducked their faces back down to the ground immediately and lay trembling.

"There's some trick to this!" he thundered.

Girl trembled, too, but stood her ground. "Sir," she reminded him quietly, "what can you keep, even after giving it to someone else?"

The Black Lord sighed. "Ah, yes," he said, "my word. And I shall keep it." And he clapped his hands once.

The biggest guard of all stepped forward. This one was twice the size of the other guards and was shaved completely bald. But, fierce as he was, he bowed meekly to his master, his forehead touching the ground.

"Free the boy," commanded the Black Lord. "Bring him up from my dungeon and give him to this girl." He indicated Girl with a wave of his hand.

He turned to Girl. "Take the accursed boy, then, and flee the city before I, the great Black Lord, ruler of all about me, change my mind."

But when Girl had followed the guard as far as the curtained doorway, he called out. "Wait!"

Fearing the worst, Girl turned to face him, but he only said, "You can't leave without telling me the answer. What *is* your name?" He added plaintively, "I won't be able to sleep unless I know."

Now what? The Black Lord will be furious with me if he learns I don't have a proper name at all, worried Girl. He'll believe I tricked him. She thought hard and said finally, "Oh Great One, I will tell my name . . ." The Black Lord leaned forward on his throne. All the courtiers lifted up their heads and looked at her expectantly. ". . . to the guardian of the gate, after the boy and I have left the palace safely," she finished.

The dark man on the black throne scowled, then he smiled. Finally he sat back and laughed loudly. All the court laughed, too, although they were not sure exactly what was funny.

"It is as I said before," the Black Lord chuckled, "you are a smart girl. Yes, you may tell your name to the guardian of the gate."

Then his smile disappeared and was replaced by a deepening frown. "But," he roared, "I warned you about acting *too* smart! Begone!"

IRL FLED, FOLLOWING THE GUARD OUT THE CURTAINED
doorway and through onyx halls to a cedar door that was set into the
black marble floor. They had arrived back at the first intersection between the
two corridors. The two guards whom Girl had bribed with silver rings still stood
at attention.

"Well, if it isn't the little thing who wanted into the throne room," chuckled
one, "and still alive, too."

"But not yet out of harm's way," added the other. "She still hasn't left the
palace. And the Black Lord may change his mind at any minute. He does that,
you know."

This interchange did not make Girl feel any more secure. "Please, sir," she
asked the bald giant, "how far is it to the dungeon?"

The huge guard only pointed wordlessly to the wooden door set into the
marble. In its center was a large brass ring. Grasping it firmly, he pulled, and the
door swung open slowly, revealing steps that led even farther down into the
earth. He motioned for her to wait.

"Can't I come with you?" asked Girl. "Why don't you answer me?"

The giant only shook his head and descended the steps. Soon he was gone
from view.

The other guards laughed. "He can't speak," explained one.

"His tongue has been cut out," added the other, "so that he can never tell anyone what is down there in the deepest dungeons from which no one has ever emerged."

Girl shivered at what was said. She wanted to tell them that they were wrong, that Boy would emerge alive from that terrible place, but she was too frightened to speak. Instead, she listened to the mute guard's heavy footsteps under the floor. The sound of his feet grew fainter and fainter, and soon faded away completely. She waited. And even the guards waited, curious to see if, for the first time ever, someone would climb out of there alive.

Finally Girl heard—oh, so faintly!—sounds far below. The sounds grew louder and more distinct. Footsteps, and two sets of them! They grew louder than the sound of her thumping heart as the giant climbed the steps, followed by Boy.

But what a changed Boy he was! The lively, talkative Boy she remembered from only a short time ago was much subdued. His eyes, very wide and solemn, peered from a face that showed pale beneath many layers of dirt. His clothes fell in tatters, and something else about him, which Girl couldn't quite make out at first, had changed. Then she saw what it was.

"You've outgrown your clothes!" she exclaimed.

"Oh, shut up!" snarled Boy. Then he looked down. "I'm sorry," he whispered. "Thank you for rescuing me."

The two guards watched, open-mouthed. "Well, I'll be," muttered one. "She's done it. The boy has really gone free."

"Not yet he hasn't," added the other, "not till they're outside the palace walls." And to the children he said, "Better hurry. And don't look back!"

Holding tight to each other's hand, Boy and Girl followed the corridor as it sloped upwards toward what they hoped would be the way out. No one else stood in their way, and after what seemed to them an eternity, they approached the great carved door through which Girl had entered the palace. Boy pushed it open, using all his strength, and they walked through, toward the strange, barren garden that lay beyond.

As they crossed the threshold, a chilling sound echoed up the corridors. It was the Black Lord, laughing in the throne room. His laughter seemed to say to

Girl: *Go, little ones. Taste your freedom while you can, for I am patient. I can wait. In the end, the Black Lord will claim you, and you will be mine once again.*

Then the massive door shut behind them and the terrible sound of laughter ceased. As soon as Girl heard the click of the closing door, she dared to speak once more. She turned to Boy and shouted, "Run!"

And before the two guards at the palace entrance had a chance to stop them, the children ducked under the crossed spears and fled down the long path of dark flagstones, past the grinning skulls imbedded in the sand on either side. They shoved at the gate, it opened for them, and they were outside the palace grounds.

Fetcher, who had lain patiently in front of the wall, leaped up and yipped, his tail wagging joyously. Boy gave the dog a big hug, while Fetcher licked his face. Then Boy stood up. "Let's go, Fetcher!"

Remembering her promise to the Black Lord, Girl called over her shoulder to the guardian of the gate, "Tell your Lord that my name is Girl, and that is the only name I have!" Then she followed Boy and Fetcher. With the dog leading the way, the three ran down the winding streets of the city.

They ran through the maze of dusty, brown streets. They turned corners, and still more corners. Soon they arrived at a house that Girl thought they had passed already, but since Boy and Fetcher seemed to know the way, she decided she was mistaken. After all, she reasoned, the mud-brick houses *did* all look the same to her.

"Wait!" Boy cried finally. He leaned against a wall, panting, while Fetcher, who was far ahead, whirled about and trotted back.

Girl ran up to Boy. "Is something wrong?"

"We're lost. I don't know the way back to the city gate," Boy declared wretchedly.

Girl panicked a moment but then remembered the map, still tucked into her sash. She unrolled it and saw immediately that Kish was no longer represented as a big square. Instead, it had become a diagram that clearly laid out the city blocks, the palace of Ur-Zababa, the temple of the dreamers, the marketplace, and the gates. And not far from the palace, a big red X and the

words YOU ARE HERE were written. Next to them was an arrow, which pointed towards the gates. Above the arrow, Girl read: TO THE EGRESS.

Girl looked around at the streets going off in all directions, then looked at the map again. "It's this way!" she pointed, and the three continued on their way.

The route took them past the temple of dreamers, its blue and red tiles gleaming in the sun. Girl caught a whiff of the incense that floated down the marble steps, and she increased her speed.

They fled through empty streets until they reached the marketplace where shoppers ambled about as before, browsing and buying. Without stopping, the children and the dog threaded their way between stalls, heading for the gates just beyond. Suddenly, Girl spotted the merchant to whom she had traded her amulet for the multicolored bracelets that still jingled on her arm. A young woman, her dark curls escaping from the bright turban wound about her head and her fringed cloak worn fashionably off one shoulder, was trying on a carnelian bracelet, holding her arm up to the light. The small cat-shaped amber carving still hung on the wall behind the jewelry-laden counter.

Girl tugged Boy's arm. "There," she panted. "It's my amulet! He took it from me and gave me these bracelets in return!"

Without saying a word, or even breaking stride, Boy stripped the bracelets from Girl's arm and threw them in the startled merchant's face. In the same motion, he reached behind the counter and pulled the amulet off the wall. And with that, they resumed running.

The gates of Kish loomed in front of them. But a platoon of copper-helmeted soldiers, with copper plates sewn to their leather armor and spears raised so the armed group resembled a giant bristling porcupine, barred their way! The captain stood at the head of his troops. When he saw the two children and their dog, he raised his arm, shouting, "There is the boy! There is the girl! Don't let them get away!"

It's Ur-Zababa, of course, Girl realized. When he found out my real name, he got angry.

"It isn't fair," she cried bitterly, "to have come all this way, only to be dragged back to that dismal place. And why didn't my map warn me of this?"

Boy put a protective arm around her shoulder. "I won't let them hurt you," he whispered fiercely.

Led by their captain, the soldiers of the Black Lord advanced upon the cowering pair. Girl knew there was no place to run. She shut her eyes tightly and waited for rough hands to grab her arm. But no one touched her. Instead, she heard shouts of fear. When she opened her eyes again, she saw the army milling about in confusion. They had dropped their weapons, and some soldiers were running away. Soon more joined those who ran, and then the entire army was in flight, away from her and Boy.

But why were they running? And the next moment Girl saw an immense lioness with angry golden eyes, which had appeared seemingly out of nowhere, chasing the frightened soldiers. Then, as the platoon scattered in all directions, this great beast turned and loped towards Girl, Boy, and Fetcher. They huddled together, watching but not daring to move.

As the huge beast came nearer, Fetcher bared his teeth and growled, prepared to sacrifice his own life to defend his friends. But Girl was prompted by something in the eyes of the approaching lioness. "Hush, Fetcher. It's all right."

Fetcher whined, then quieted down apprehensively. The tawny animal walked right up to them and settled down calmly on her hind legs.

Boy, who had been holding his breath, let it all out at once. "She isn't going to eat us," he said with a good deal of relief and wonder.

"Of course not," replied Girl joyfully. "Don't you see? She's the one whom Mother fed!"

Girl put forth a tentative hand and stroked the lovely golden fur between the great ears. And the lioness purred! She almost seemed to smile. Abruptly, she stood up, stretched and yawned, showing white teeth sharp as daggers, and then sauntered off slowly.

Girl looked at Boy. Boy looked back at Girl. "Now!" they cried together.

They raced through the gates and out of the city, Fetcher at their heels. Once on the other side, they stood catching their breath and searching for Mother. The plain spread out before them, broad and brown and empty. Neither Mother nor the little goat was anywhere in sight.

DIRECTLY BEHIND BOY AND GIRL WERE THE CITY GATES, and in front of them stood a caravan, its wooden carts laden with trade goods and hitched to strong asses and oxen. There were curtained wagons, too, carrying those passengers who could afford to ride in such luxury. As Girl searched frantically for Mother, a gray, velvet paw pulled back the embroidered curtain of one wagon, and the Great Cat herself peered out at them.

"It's Mother!" cried Girl, and they scrambled into the wagon.

As Girl sat down next to her, Mother growled, "It's about time." Then she gave Girl a fierce, relieved hug. Girl rubbed her cheek gratefully into Mother's soft fur and drew back to look at her.

"Mother," she exclaimed, "you've grown smaller!"

"Silly little fish," Mother sniffed, "I'm the same size I've always been. *You've* grown *taller*."

The asses that were hitched to the wagon started up with a jolt, pitching Girl back into her seat and reminding her that they were in a caravan. "Mother, how did you get all this?" she asked, indicating the luxurious wagon in which they rode.

"I fear I had to trade our little goat in return for this passage," answered the Great Cat. "But I think she will be happier now, for she has joined a herd and no longer has to roam the plains with us. Catwalks are not for goats.

"Now," she continued, "tell me what happened in the city."

"Oh, mother," wailed Girl, "I didn't find Ramose. I don't think we will *ever* find him."

"I think you will," answered Mother quietly. "And now, tell me about the city."

Breathlessly, Girl related their adventures; how she and Boy became separated at the bazaar, and how she escaped from the temple of the dreamers. She told Mother about Fetcher leading her to the palace, how she discovered that Boy was a prisoner of the Black Lord, and how she engaged the frightful ruler in a contest of riddles to rescue her friend.

Girl paused. "But, Mother, when I couldn't solve the Black Lord's riddle, the small black cat broke the silence and gave me the answer. Did *you* have a hand in that?"

"Of course," snorted Mother. "After all, if I don't have the power to work a little magic through lesser cats, I may as well surrender my whiskers."

Then Girl added, "Oh, and thank you, too, for giving our dinner to the lioness. I know that's why she frightened off the Black Lord's soldiers and helped us escape."

"If you give to a stranger in need," Mother replied, "someday that stranger may give you what *you* need."

Boy smelled terrible. Mother made him sit at the far end of the wagon. As soon as the caravan reached the river, he hopped out, dove into the cool, clear water, and washed up. Fetcher, when he saw his best friend swimming, jumped in, too, and soon they were both clean as could be.

That night the caravan camped at a small oasis by the river's bend. A number of fires were lit, and about them were various families and travel companions. Delicious odors filled the air, including that of the fine fat duck Boy had brought down earlier in the day with his throwing stick. After dinner, he and Girl joined their caravan driver who gathered with the other drivers around one of the campfires. One man had a small flute, with which he accompanied

the others who sang songs they had learned during their travels. Girl sat, happily tired, watching and listening to the singers. Boy clapped to the music while Fetcher slept at his feet. Only when she felt she could no longer stay awake did Girl leave the singing and make her way back to their own fire, where Mother was already sleeping.

She curled up next to Mother, resting her head on the warm, gray fur, and thought sleepily, Mother calls me her little fish, but that's not my name. Those names guessed by the Black Lord—they were all good names, too. But I know that none of them are mine.

Girl was filled with the conviction that by the time the Catswalk ended she would find her true name, and that Boy would, too. Just as she drifted off to sleep, she felt Boy fastening the amulet gently around her neck.

Girl did not awaken until the sun was quite high the next morning and the caravan drivers had finished hitching their wagons. Mother had already eaten breakfast, but she saved some barley cakes for Girl.

"Yes, we ate the last of our barley cakes a long time back," explained Mother in answer to Girl's unspoken question, "but the caravan is well supplied with barley, and even honey and raisins, so that we shall not want for nourishment."

The night before, Girl had been too tired for her habitual perusal of the map, but now she unrolled and studied it as she munched on her breakfast.

"Mother!" she called out. "I can read the map! I can read it *all* now!"

Mother and Boy ran over and watched with great interest as she showed them the names of all the places they had been, and even places they hadn't been near and wouldn't be going to.

"And this is where we are going," she pointed out. "See? It's a small village by the river. And I think Ramose will be there, too."

"Ramose? Why do you think that?"

"Because right here, next to the village, is a big X. And over the X, it says HERE I AM."

Travelling with the caravan was pleasant, and much easier than walking. Heading ever northward, soon they were so far from the city that they could no longer see it, even as a blue blur on the horizon. Girl's heart was light. She knew now that soon they would reach the village where she could return Ramose's map and, thus, accomplish her mission. Sometimes she felt that her mission consisted of more than just returning the map, but she wasn't sure what else that could be.

Boy was not the only one who had outgrown his clothes. Girl's dress had become far too short, but nothing seemed much of a problem for Mother. The Great Cat found a merchant travelling with the caravan who loved barley cakes and had no wife to make them. While on the journey, Mother baked him many good batches, and in return he gave Girl a finely woven robe of white linen. A row of flowers was embroidered at the hem, and it was much finer than her dresses of undyed goat's fleece. Of course, the robe was not half so fine as the purple silk garment with which she had bribed the guard at the Black Lord's palace. But when Girl remembered the terrible price of the silk robe, she preferred her new linen one.

The merchant gave a simpler robe to Boy to replace his wretched rags, which still smelled faintly of the dungeon. Boy buried the rags and would not talk about his experiences underground. Only once did Girl bring it up, and then he quickly changed the subject, so she never mentioned it again.

Boy was very grateful for his new clothing and thanked both Mother and the merchant warmly. In fact, since his ordeal in the dungeon, he had become an altogether more reasonable person and was much easier to get along with. He tried hard to mind his manners and, at least *sometimes*, remembered to say "please" and "may I."

When the caravan reached the little village marked on the map by the x, the sun was high. The townsfolk had gathered in the village square to await the merchants' arrival and had prepared much of their produce for trade. Soon the caravan merchants briskly swapped bright bolts of fringed cloth, highly polished brass pots, and carven ivory combs for clay jugs of date wine, hard balls of goat cheese, and great jars of barley and olive oil.

But Girl went in search of the little hut that had been marked on her map with an x. She found it quickly enough. There, outside of a round, mud-plastered house, not unlike the home she had left so long ago, sat Ramose on a three-legged stool in the sun. He was smoking a clay pipe, and when he saw Girl, he took one last slow puff and laid it down.

"Ramose! Remember me? Look, I've brought your map." And she held out the parchment.

But he only commented mildly, "Took your good time getting here, didn't you?"

This annoyed Girl immensely. After all she had been through! "Mother and I," she began angrily, "crossed the great plain just to bring this to you, and . . ."

"But that's not *my* map. I left it for *you*. Didn't you read the note on the back?"

"A note?" Girl turned the map over. Sure enough, there it was. "That's funny," she mused. "I never noticed it before."

"Perhaps," suggested Ramose, "that's because you couldn't *read* it until now."

Girl read the note aloud. "Dear Reader," she began. (Why, she thought, that's *me*!)

She continued:

> KINDLY ACCEPT, O BEST BELOVED, AND USE WISELY THIS PRICELESS MAP OF LIFE. BE NOT FOOLED OR MISLED BY IMITATIONS! ONLY THIS, THE ORIGINAL MAP OF LIFE, WHEN CORRECTLY READ, UNDERSTOOD, AND FOLLOWED CAN CARRY ALL SWEET YOUNG GIRLS (AND BOYS, TOO, SHOULD THEY ELECT TO COME) DIRECTLY ALONG THE ROAD TO MATURITY. THE MAP OF LIFE CAN LEAD THE USER SAFELY PAST ALL TEMPTATIONS, LURES, ENTICEMENTS, ETC., STRAIGHTAWAY ON THE PATH OF LEARNING AND WISDOM, AND WILL TURN GIRLS INTO WOMEN, BOYS INTO MEN, AND PUPPIES INTO FULL-GROWN DOGS. (CATS, BEING WISE ALREADY, NEED NO MAP.)

And on the bottom she read, "P.S. WE HOPE YOU WERE CAREFUL IN THE CITY!"

Girl looked up from the map. "Does this mean I'm grown up now?"

"Of course you are. I thought you already knew that," said a voice behind her.

She turned around; Boy stood there. Only, she thought, he's become a young man and I didn't realize it. Really, she continued to herself, he makes a

63

much better-looking young man than he did a boy. His ears don't stick out so much now.

Ramose dug in the folds of his garment and produced a polished silver mirror. He held it up to her. "See for yourself."

Girl gazed into the surface. A beautiful young woman smiled back at her from dark, almond-shaped eyes.

"The minute I emerged from the dungeon, I could see that you had grown," announced Boy.

By this time, Mother had joined the group. "Tell her the rest," she said to Boy.

"I have a new name now," the young man announced proudly. "Fetcher helped me earn it, and he'll always be my friend. Together we caught food for you and Mother on the journey, and thus my name is Hunter."

"That's a good name," answered the young woman who had been Girl, "and now I have a new name, too." She smiled mischievously. "The Black Lord couldn't guess my name. Can you?"

Hunter pondered for a moment. "Well, I would call you Beautiful," he ventured. "In fact, come to think of it, I would call you Beloved. And I would like to call you my wife, if that's all right with you."

Girl blushed. It had never occurred to her that Hunter might consider her beautiful, beloved, or his wife, but for some reason this made her happy. She thought it over, "You may call me all those names, because I like them. But I have more. I helped us find our way by learning to read the map, so my name is Reader. I beat the Black Lord in a guessing game, so my name is Riddler. And I saved you from the deep dungeon, which makes me Rescuer."

Then she smiled. "But the note on the back of my map addressed me as Beloved, and that will be my proper name."

Mother spoke up. "Little fish, you have always been my Beloved."

"And a perfect name it is," announced Ramose. "In fact, they are *all* perfect names. But I must be on my way now." And he turned to leave.

"Oh, no!" protested Beloved. "Please don't leave so soon! Won't you at least share our dinner with us?"

Ramose bowed low. "Dear princess, I only waited to keep your house for you until you arrived to claim it." With a sweep of his arm, he indicated the little hut.

"Is this *our* house now?" Beloved peeked in through the open door.

Inside, the one-room hut looked very similar to the one in which she had been raised. The clean floor was of packed earth, and a little broom of rushes leaned against the wall. A hole in the ceiling right above the open hearth would allow the smoke to escape. Beloved knew that at night she would look through the hole at the moon and the stars.

This might very well be my old home, she realized, except that it stands on the outskirts of the village, and I grew up all alone but for Mother by the river's edge.

"Of course it's your house," Ramose replied. "After all, you can't go all the way *back* again."

S O BELOVED SETTLED INTO HER NEW HOUSE WITH HUNTER,

Mother, and Fetcher. She and the Great Cat planted a small garden. Both Beloved and Hunter helped Mother weed and water the garden and harvest the grains and vegetables. Chickens scratched near the door. Pretty soon they got a small goat, too. Some days Hunter and Fetcher went off and returned with meat for the table.

Hunter, who was good with wood, built a cart for the goat to pull, and when the garden produced more vegetables than they could eat, they took the produce to the marketplace in the village square. At the market, they exchanged the surplus food for supplies they needed: polished copper pots and clay jars, bolts of fine cloth, sharp stone axes for chopping wood, and even two silver flutes so they could make music.

One day Beloved returned from the market with a mirror and a tiny pot of green paint for her eyelids. When Mother saw Beloved's painted eyes, she started to say something and then thought better of it. For she remembered that Beloved was no longer a girl, and that it was quite proper, now, for her to paint her eyelids.

And as time went by, one, two, and finally three babies crawled and toddled about the floor of the little hut.

Between them, Beloved and Hunter learned to do the things that Mother had done for Beloved when she was a girl. Beloved even learned how to make

barley cakes just as delicious as Mother's. This meant that Mother didn't have to spend as much time at home, so she began going out for long stretches at a time. One evening she failed to return for dinner, which vexed Beloved, who had prepared a delicious duck with date sauce, and worried her, too.

When Mother returned later that night, she reassured Beloved. "Don't worry about me. And I, a Great Cat, will always find food. I was out, seeing what I could see."

And the next night Mother didn't return until after the whole family had gone to bed. Beloved, who couldn't fall asleep because she was concerned, heard Mother come in quietly and curl up with the sleeping babies. The next morning the Great Cat said nothing.

There came a time when Mother stayed away for three days in a row. Although she had been told not to worry, Beloved was wild with anxiety. Hunter tried to comfort her.

"Remember, Mother is the last of the Great Cats. If she has stayed away, she must have a good reason."

Beloved was in tears. "But what if she fell into the river and was eaten by a crocodile?" she sobbed. "Or a lion?"

Hunter wiped away her tears. "Certainly not a lion. You *know* lions are Mother's friends."

Just then, Mother marched in, carrying a big basket which she handed to Beloved. In the basket, five kittens curled up together into one fuzzy, gray ball. Beloved's tears stopped as she stared at the little mewing things.

"These are mine," Mother told her, "and my gift to you. Do not expect them to speak, for they are lesser cats. As soon as they are old enough, I must go away on a Catswalk."

Beloved began to cry again upon hearing this news. "But Mother, we already went on a Catswalk," she protested, "and anyway, we need you to stay here with us!"

Mother took Beloved's hand between her two velvety gray paws. "You don't *really* need me anymore, little fish. I have done my job well, and now you can do everything I once did for you.

"Of course," she added thoughtfully, "you'll never be as wise as me, but after all, you're not a Great Cat. And as for the Catswalk, that was *your* Catswalk. Now it's time for me to go on my *own* Catswalk."

SO BELOVED HAD TO LET MOTHER GO BECAUSE SHE KNEW
what the Great Cat said was true. But she insisted that Mother take along
a big basket filled with goat cheese and barley cakes, baked in the way the Great
Cat had taught her. She and Hunter and their three children lined up outside
the house to wave good-bye. Even Fetcher, who sensed that it was a solemn
occasion, stood quietly and watched.

Beloved didn't stop watching as Mother strode farther and farther away,
every now and then turning to wave to the family. Soon Mother had gone such
a distance that Beloved had to squint in order to see her at all. Then something
strange happened. It seemed to Beloved that Ramose stepped out from behind
a clump of palm trees and joined the Great Cat. The two turned and waved. Then
Mother took Ramose's arm and they continued on.

"Hunter," exclaimed Beloved, "that was Ramose! Did you see?"

Hunter squinted, frowning. "I don't see a thing. Perhaps the sun was in
your eyes."

Beloved blinked, shook her head, and looked again. But Mother and
Ramose, if indeed they had been there together, had disappeared from sight.

At first, Beloved thought Mother might return from her Catswalk, and she
always set an extra plate in case the Great Cat came back hungry. But as the
years passed, she realized that Mother had gone for good. The kittens became
cats and watched the children grow up. Because of her love and respect for

Mother, Beloved taught her children to love and respect all cats even if, being lesser cats, they couldn't speak.

Since Beloved was also Reader, it was natural for her to become Writer and to write down the adventures she had had with Mother and Hunter. Every night she read stories to her children about the wonderful but terrible city of Kish; her riddle contest with Ur-Zababa, the Black Lord, in his fearsome black palace beneath the earth; of the lioness who saved her and Hunter's lives; and of Mother, wise and good, the last of the Great Cats. Beloved taught her family to read, so when they grew up and had children of their own, they could read these stories to them.

But after Mother, no cat ever talked.

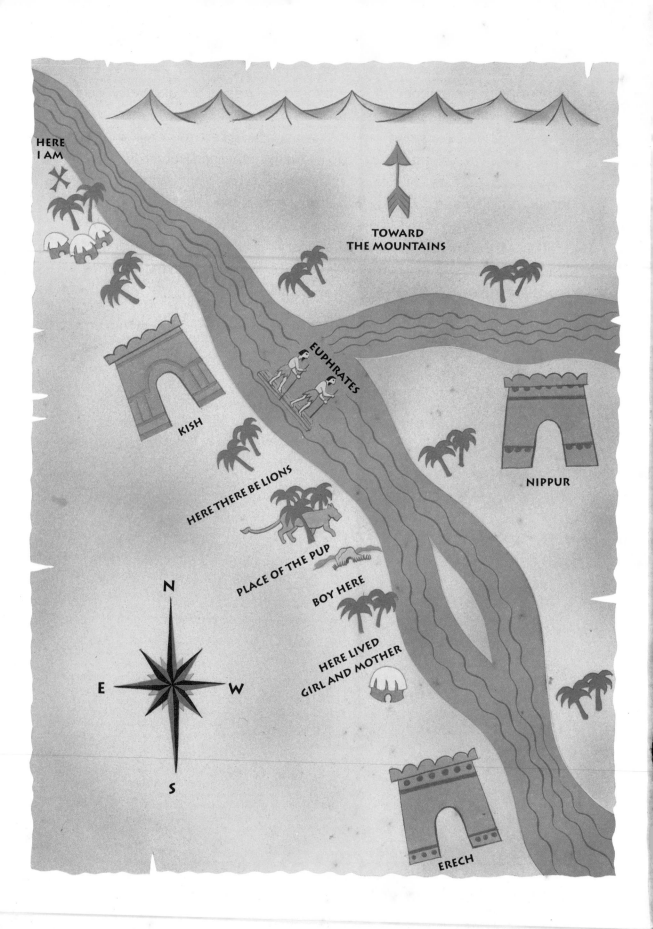